IC Tillwo
lworth, Mary
s time for ballet! /
.99

DISCARD

3 4028 09579 8477
HARRIS COUNTY PUBLIC LIBRARY

O9-BTL-592

...OR BALLET!

Adapted by **Mary Tillworth**
Illustrated by **MJ Illustrations**
Cover illustration colored by **Steve Talkowski**

Based on the teleplay "The Super Ballet Bowl!" by Tim McKeon, Jonny Belt, and Robert Scull

A Random House PICTUREBACK® Book

Random House 🏠 New York

© 2015 Viacom International Inc. All rights reserved. Published in the United States by Random House Children's Books, a division of Penguin Random House LLC, 1745 Broadway, New York, NY 10019, and in Canada by Random House of Canada, a division of Penguin Random House Ltd., Toronto. Pictureback, Random House, and the Random House colophon are registered trademarks of Penguin Random House LLC. Nickelodeon, Bubble Guppies, and all related titles, logos, and characters are trademarks of Viacom International Inc.
randomhousekids.com
ISBN 978-0-553-52117-7
MANUFACTURED IN CHINA
10 9 8 7 6 5 4 3 2 1

Molly and Gil were on their way to school one morning when they heard beautiful music. They followed the sweet sound to a backyard with a large television.

"We're watching a ballet performance of 'Mary Had a Little Lamb'!" cheered a ballet fan.

Molly was enchanted. "I want to be a ballerina!" she said.

"Ballet is beautiful!" Molly told her class.

"I love ballet," said Oona, "because you get to wear a tutu!"

Mr. Grouper smiled. "And you also wear special shoes called slippers."

"Let's think about ballet!" said Mr. Grouper. "Ballet dancers perform in lots of places, like on a . . ."

"Stage!" said Deema.

Mr. Grouper smiled. "That's right! And ballet music is played with instruments, such as a . . ."

"Piano!" suggested Goby. "Or a flute! Or a violin!"

The Bubble Guppies pretended they were ballet dancers. They dressed in costumes from famous ballets and twirled around.

Then Mr. Grouper took the Guppies to a ballet class, where they learned how to leap, jump, pirouette, and plié. They also learned different ballet positions.

The Guppies were having so much fun dancing that they decided to enter the Super Ballet Bowl, a huge ballet like the one Molly and Gil had seen on TV!

On the night of the Super Ballet Bowl, fans gathered at the stadium for the Bubble Guppies' performance of *Aliens Versus the Princess.* As the curtains opened, Prince Gil, along with the castle guards, Goby and Nonny, danced onto the stage.

The crowd oohed and aahed as Princess Molly appeared, wearing a beautiful golden crown. Prince Gil took her hand, and they danced a lovely duet.

When night fell onstage, the prince and princess went to sleep. And so did the castle guards!

Deep in the night, two aliens tiptoed onto the stage and took Princess Molly's crown.

The royal kingdom awoke to find the princess's crown missing! They searched for the culprits and found the two guilty aliens as they were about to leave in their spaceship.

The prince, princess, and guards chased the aliens.
One of the aliens threw the crown high into the air. Princess Molly
saw her chance. She leapt up and soared toward her crown!

Prince Gil knew that his princess had to make a safe landing.
He raced down the field to catch her.

Harris County Public Library, Houston, TX

Princess Molly caught the crown, and Prince Gil caught the princess! It was a happy ending to a great story, and a super ballet at the Super Ballet Bowl!